P9-CPZ-855

Bertolt

Jacques Goldstyn

For my father Michel, who taught me how
to climb trees and how to draw.

Translated from the French by
Claudia Zoe Bedrick

www.enchantedlionbooks.com

First American Edition published in 2017 by Enchanted Lion Books,
67 West Street, Unit 317A, Brooklyn, New York 11222
English-language translation copyright © 2017 by Claudia Zoe Bedrick
English-language edition copyright © 2017 by Enchanted Lion Books
Originally published in Canada by Les Editions de la Pasteque © 2015 as L'Arbragan
All rights reserved under International and Pan-American Copyright Conventions
A CIP record is on file with the Library of Congress
ISBN: 978-1-59270-229-9
Printed in China by RR Donnelley Asia Printing Solutions

First Printing

Bertolt

Jacques Goldstyn

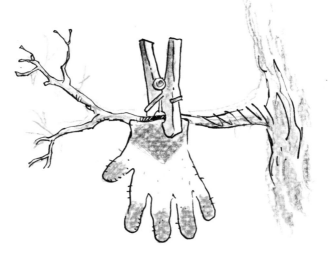

ENCHANTED LION BOOKS
NEW YORK

Darn, darn, and more darn.
Where's my mitten?
I don't see it anywhere.

I know. I'll go to the Lost & Found.
There are tons of gloves there.
Leather ones. Wool mittens.
Even baseball gloves.

My mitten wasn't there, so I took one
that doesn't match. Who cares.
I like it this way. Wearing two
different mittens is kind of funny.

The only problem is that when you're different,
people can laugh at you, or even worse.
Sometimes people don't like what's different.

To tell you the truth,
I have a feeling I'm not like other people.
Not just because of the mittens.

Most people do things together
all the time.

Like Mr. Buvard and his friends.

Or the Berman brothers.

Or Ms. Brock and her knitting club.

Or Ana-Marie and her friends.

But me—I'm what you call a loner.
I do stuff all by myself,
and it doesn't bother me one bit.
Just the opposite.

I love doing lots of things
by myself, but I love climbing
my tree best of all.

Bertolt.

That's the name of my tree.

Bertolt is an ancient oak. I know this because
one day workers came to cut down another oak.
I counted its rings and got 172 years.

163
164
165
166
167
168
169
170
171
172

Bertolt is much bigger.
He must be at least 500 years old.

I love everything about Bertolt,
but when spring arrives his leaves
make the coolest hideout ever.
It's like a cave, a maze, and a fortress!

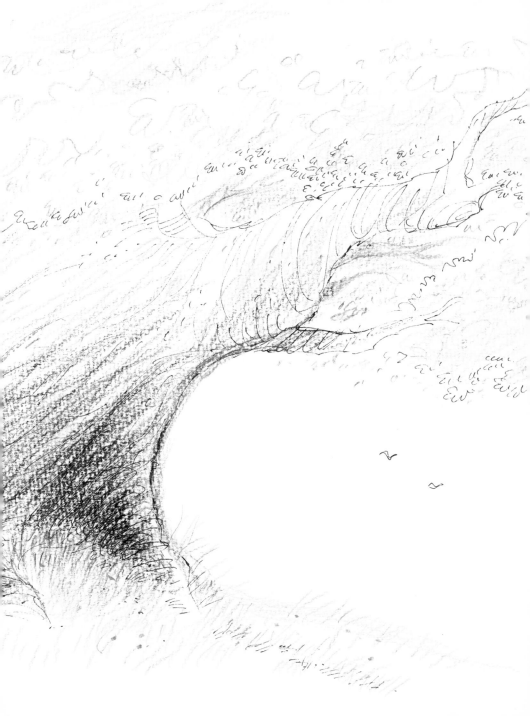

No one else climbs Bertolt.
Maybe they haven't thought of it.
Or maybe they're scared.
Anyone can climb an ordinary tree,
but an old oak is something else.

The first branch must be 15 feet from the ground.
To reach it, you have to go up the trunk,
which is like a wall. But I know all of Bertolt's hollows
and where to put my hands and feet.
It's like climbing up a secret ladder.

Once I reach the first branch,
I continue to climb.

It's like going up a steep, winding road,
so forget it if you get dizzy.

When Bertolt is covered with leaves, nobody can see
me, but I can see everyone else.

I can see Marie, the lawyer's daughter, kissing Kevin.

And the Tucker twins, who steal bottles from the grocer
and sell them back to him.

I can see the postman setting his traps.

And Cynthia eating corn.

I'm never alone in my tree.
Squirrels scamper in search of acorns.

There's a really smart crow
who's become my friend.

There's an old owl
who sleeps all day.
I respect him a lot.

There are cicadas whose songs
are 100 decibels!

And there are
nuthatches,

cardinals,

and buntings.

There are also some friendly bees, but don't annoy them, not even for a second.

I know everything about Bertolt.

When I climb way up high, I can see for miles around.

When it storms, my tree is an amazing place.
I have to hold on really tight so I won't blow away.
It always surprises me to see the wind press
the reeds straight down to the ground.

On these days, I take shelter deep inside Bertolt's branches,
which sway and creak like the masts of a big ship.

I love spring storms.

I can't wait for spring!

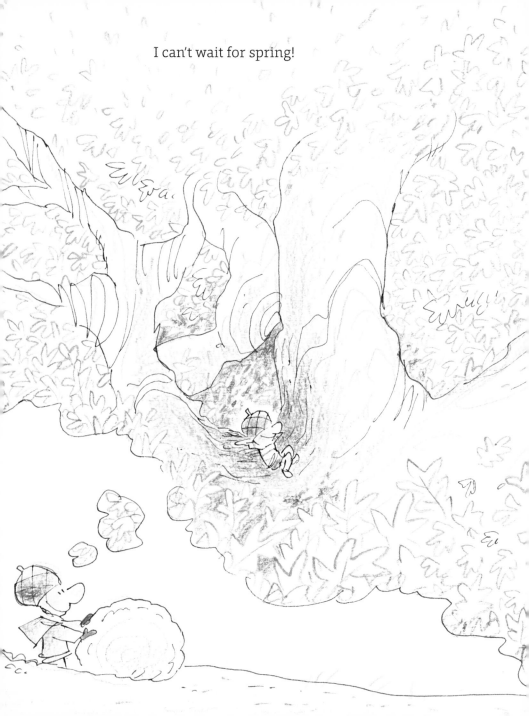

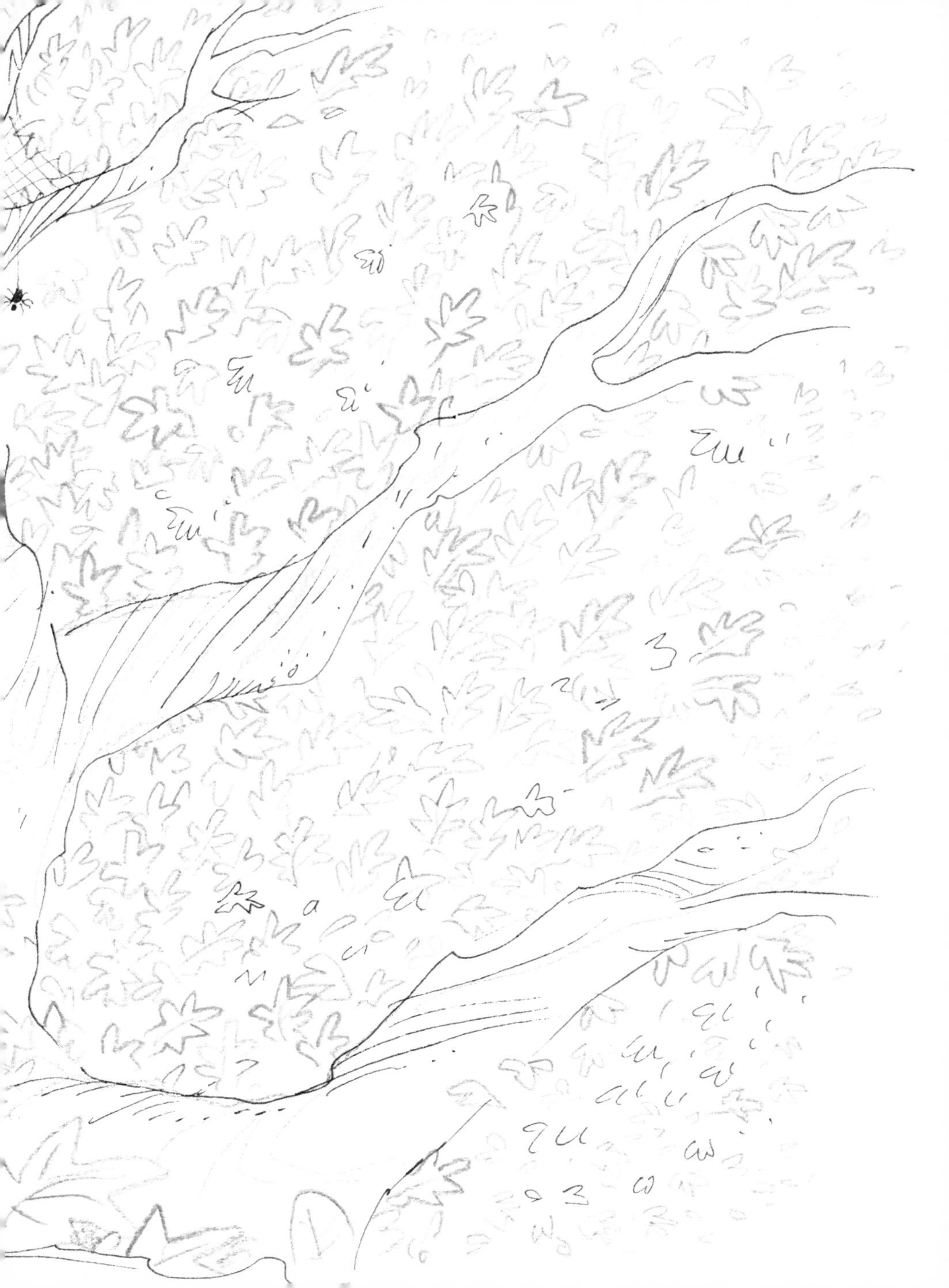

Hooray!

All at once, the trees burst into bloom.

The lime.

The elm.

The flowering plum.

The weeping willow.

All except Bertolt.

RADFORD PUBLIC LIBRARY
30 WEST MAIN STREET
RADFORD, VA 24141
540-731-3621

Days pass. Then weeks.
I wait. I hope. I pray.
But finally I have to accept it.
Bertolt is dead.

When a cat dies,
we know it right away.

Same with a bird.

But with a tree, it's hard to tell.
A tree just stands there like a huge,
boney creature that's sleeping
or playing a trick on us.

If Bertolt had been killed by lightening or cut down,

I would have understood.

I know what to do when a cat or a bird dies.
But what should I do for Bertolt?

I have to do something before Bertolt is turned into firewood, furniture, or toothpicks.

I think I have an idea.

school

school